Paddington
at St Paul's

For more activities, games, books and fun, visit www.paddington.com

First published in hardback by HarperCollins Children's Books in 2018

1 3 5 7 9 10 8 6 4 2

ISBN: 978-0-00-827204-3

HarperCollins Children's Books is a division of HarperCollins Publishers Ltd.

Text copyright © Michael Bond 2018
Illustrations copyright © R. W. Alley 2018

Visit our website at: www.harpercollins.co.uk

Printed in Spain

Michael Bond
Paddington
at St Paul's

Illustrated by R. W. Alley

HarperCollins *Children's Books*

Most mornings Paddington called in at Mr Gruber's antique shop in the Portobello Market in order to share his elevenses, but one day his friend telephoned and suggested he should come in earlier.

It was most unusual, and for once Paddington didn't collect the buns from the nearby bakers on his way in.

"I was thinking the other day," said Mr Gruber, "what with Buckingham Palace and the Houses of Parliament you must have had your fill of famous buildings you can see from outside, but that's as far as it goes."

"I nearly got my head stuck in the railings at Buckingham Palace," said Paddington.

"Well, there you are," said Mr Gruber.
"It's not ideal." He paused for thought.
"One of my regular customers happens
to be a taxi driver and he came up
with an interesting idea. Not only
did he suggest a place to visit,
but he said that the next
fine day he would take
us there."

He broke off with
a twinkle in his eyes
at the sound of
a vehicle drawing
up outside.

"I'll tell you something," said the taxi driver as Paddington scrambled in. "The place I'm taking you to took thirty-five years to build and I'm willing to bet it's bigger and better than anywhere else you've seen."

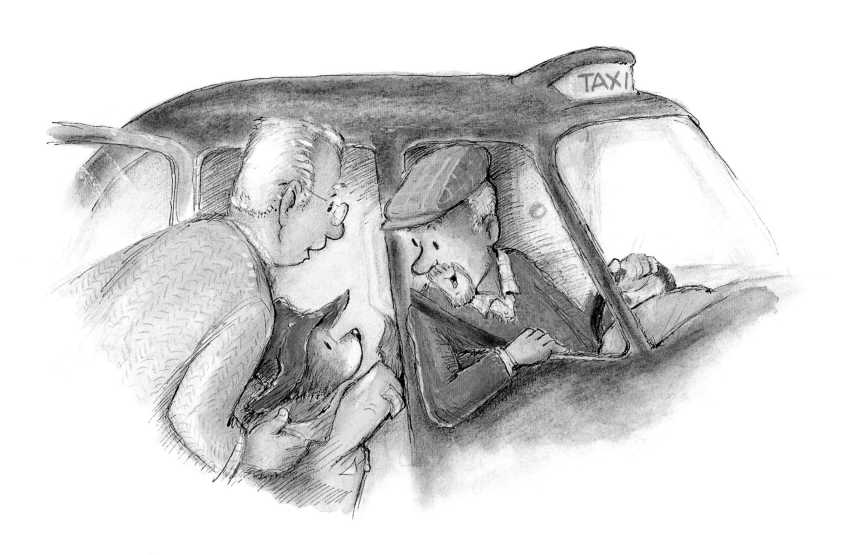

"I expect they used the same builders as the ones who repaired our roof," exclaimed Paddington. "Mr Brown says the job took three times as long as it should have done."

"I don't think they were around in those days," chuckled Mr Gruber. "This building was designed by Sir Christopher Wren soon after the Great Fire of London in 1666."

"Visitors are welcome," he continued, "and provided there isn't a special event taking place you can explore every nook and cranny to your heart's content."

"Only mind you don't get lost," said the taxi driver.

"I've brought a whistle for him," said Mr Gruber. "Two blasts on it and I'll be there."

Paddington felt very important as they
worked their way through the early morning traffic.
   Best of all, he made good use of the whistle before they
reached their destination and it worked a treat.

"This is St Paul's Cathedral," said the taxi driver as they
drew up outside an enormous building. "The part I like best
is called the Whispering Gallery. It's right up inside the dome,
thirty metres above the ground floor, but if you know the right
people there's a lift and the view is marvellous. Ask for Ellie.
She's a nice girl and she'll look after you."

The taxi driver was as good as his word. As soon as they'd found Ellie she led them straight to the lift.

On the way up, Mr Gruber explained to Paddington how the Whispering Gallery got its name. "They say if you speak very quietly against the wall, someone can hear what you are saying all the way across on the other side."

"I don't think those people can have read the signs," hissed Paddington, as they stepped out of the lift. He glared at the couple sitting nearby. Far from whispering, they were in the middle of a loud argument about the number of steps there were between them and the ground floor. The man said it was 239 and the lady said it felt like many more than that – especially in high heels.

Paddington gave each of them a hard stare before turning his attention to the view below.

Having gazed for a moment or two as though he couldn't believe his eyes, Paddington suddenly blew several warning blasts on his whistle before making a dash for the stairs.

Mr Gruber took a glance before he followed on and, to his astonishment, on the floor below him a group of school children were lying on their backs staring up at the sky. It was no wonder Paddington wanted to investigate what was going on.

By the time Mr Gruber caught up with him, Paddington had joined the children on the floor.

"It's all right, Mr Gruber," called Paddington as he caught sight of his friend's worried expression. "I'm just admiring the view. "Only I think a pigeon must be sitting on the roof," he added. "I can't see very much."

Mr Gruber recalled reading that if you lay on your back you could see right up through the Golden Gallery and on through the Ball and Lantern at the very top of the building some 111 metres from the Cathedral floor.

"I think you may need to fold back the brim of your hat, Mr Brown," suggested Mr Gruber helpfully. "Perhaps we have seen as much as we can from here. It's time we explored what goes on below stairs."

THIS WAY TO THE CRYPT

And, as ever, he was right. It was like entering another world. Apart from the fact that over the years it had been an area where many famous people such as Sir Winston Churchill had been laid to rest, all manner of things took place there from a rehearsal room for choir boys to a shopping centre with its own bookshop, a tea room and a café.

"Their buns look almost as good as the ones at the bakers in the Portobello Road," said Paddington, licking his lips as he caught sight of a display in one of the cabinets.

"So they do, Mr Brown," replied Mr Gruber. "In fact," he added, glancing at his watch, "it's almost time for our elevenses."

Unfortunately, it seemed as though a lot of other people had the same idea because the queue stretched rather a long way.

"I tell you what, Mr Brown," suggested Mr Gruber. "Why don't you go to the shop over there to see if you can find a postcard for your Aunt Lucy while I stay here to get our buns and cocoa."

Paddington needed no second bidding and he hurried off towards the shop. He'd almost reached the postcard stand when there was a sudden commotion and, before he knew what was happening, he found himself being swept off his feet by a crowd of young boys all heading in the opposite direction.

Deciding this was definitely another one of his emergencies, Paddington gave an extra hard blast on his whistle.

"Wow!" exclaimed one of the boys as they all piled into what appeared to be some sort of changing room. "You've just hit a top C. The choirmaster will be most impressed."

"Are you new?" asked another, looking at Paddington curiously.

"Hurry up, we're going to be late!" exclaimed a third boy before Paddington had time to answer. "Quick, you'll need to wear a surplice," he added, handing Paddington an outfit identical to the one he had just put on over his own clothes.

"You won't be allowed to wear that," said the first boy, removing Paddington's hat and hanging it on a peg.

If the choirmaster was surprised at the sight of the new chorister, it was as nothing compared with his reaction when they began to sing.

"I'm sorry," said Paddington as everyone stopped and all eyes were turned in his direction. "I seem to be having trouble reading my music. I think someone must have spilled some ink because it's covered all over in black spots."

Fortunately, the choirmaster was a kindly gentleman and, once the confusion had been explained, he was very understanding. He even let Paddington sit with the boys in the choir stalls when they sang upstairs in the Cathedral, although he did suggest Mr Gruber should hold onto the whistle for safekeeping.

"There can't be many bears who have sung with the choir in St Paul's," chuckled Mr Gruber as they returned to Windsor Gardens in a taxi later that day.

"I'm not sure they were very impressed with my arpeggios," said Paddington sadly.

"I think it may have had something to do with the fact that the whistle can only play one note," explained Mr Gruber. "But it was a very special note though, Mr Brown," he added tactfully as he looked fondly at his friend.

"You're going to have a lot to say to Aunt Lucy when you write to tell her all about your visit to St Paul's," said Mr Gruber as the taxi drew up outside number thirty-two Windsor Gardens.

"It's lucky Ellie gave me one of their giant books
of postcards when we left," agreed Paddington.
"It was such a special outing I don't think I'm going
to manage to fit it all onto one card."